Jamie Jaworski

P9-DFG-654

THE
LEMONADE TRICK

Other Apple Paperbacks
by SCOTT CORBETT:

The Hangman's Ghost Trick
The Hairy Horror Trick
The Disappearing Dog Trick
The Mailbox Trick

THE LEMONADE TRICK

Scott Corbett

Illustrated by Paul Galdone

AN
APPLE
PAPERBACK

SCHOLASTIC INC.

New York Toronto London Auckland Sydney

No part of this publication may be reproduced in whole or in part, or stored in a retrieval system, or transmitted in any form or by any means, electronic, mechanical, photocopying, recording, or otherwise, without written permission of the publisher. For information regarding permission, write to Little, Brown and Company, 34 Beacon Street, Boston, MA 02106.

ISBN 0-590-32197-8

Copyright ©1960 by Scott Corbett. All rights reserved. Published by Scholastic Inc., 730 Broadway, New York, NY 10003, by arrangement with Little, Brown and Company. APPLE PAPERBACKS is a registered trademark of Scholastic Inc.

12 11 10 9 8 7 6 5 4   0 1 2 3/9

Printed in the U.S.A.   11

First Scholastic printing, January 1988

To BILL PIERCE

Our Family's Top Producer

THE LEMONADE TRICK

1

PETERSON PARK was a small public park, but it seemed large to Kerby Maxwell — especially when he was at the far end of it and already late for supper.

Kerby often had this trouble. When he was playing in the park he tended to forget about time, until finally he would notice that the sunlight had grown red-golden in color and the air was cooler and the shadows were longer. Then he would jump up (if he were wrestling a friend) or jump down (if he were climbing a tree) and find some grown-up to ask what time it was.

Running over to an old gentleman sitting on a park bench, Kerby asked, "Can you tell me what time it is, please, mister?"

The old gentleman hauled out a pocket watch on a silver chain.

"Five minutes after six," he announced.

"Five after? Gosh! Well, thanks anyway, mister."

Kerby was already five minutes late.

He turned and whistled to his dog. Waldo was still more of an overgrown puppy than a regular dog, and not yet trained very well about a lot of things. Still, he often obeyed Kerby, especially when he felt like it.

"Come on!" cried Kerby, and rushed away with Waldo bounding at his heels. The boy ran as fast as he could, keeping an eye out for such everyday dangers as strange dogs, grown-ups who would get in his way and then tell him to watch where he was going, and Bumps Burton.

Bumps Burton lived next to the vacant lot behind Kerby's house. He was large for his age, and clumsy. He was not very smart in school. Nobody liked him, because he was a big bully. He made a regular hobby of twisting small boys' noses. He considered a day wasted when he didn't twist at least two or three. Occasionally he twisted an ear for good measure.

The only good thing you could say for Bumps was, he never hit a boy smaller than himself. Just twisted noses. And ears. Kerby's had been between Bumps's cruel fingers more than once. Kerby did not intend to find them there again if he could help it.

As he rounded a curve in the path, he pulled up short. Alongside the path not far from the drinking fountain was a drain with a small iron grating over it. An old lady had the heel of her shoe caught in the drain.

4

"Oh! Oh! Help me, someone," she was saying.

She was a strange-looking old lady. Her hat was large and had an enormous feather trailing from it. She wore a draggly black cape over a draggly black dress — and high-heeled shoes, which hardly seemed the right thing for such an old lady to be wearing.

"Here, little boy! Will you help me, please?"

Even though he was late for supper, Kerby said, "Yes, ma'am," and hurried forward. The old lady took her foot out of the shoe and stood balancing herself on one foot while Kerby bent down and pulled at the shoe.

"Careful, don't spoil it!" said the old lady. "The trouble is, this new fashion of having such small spiky heels is bad," she grumbled. "Bad, bad, bad."

Kerby worked the shoe loose, and she put her foot back into it.

"Thank you. Thank you very much," she said, in a voice that made her sound a bit like a trained crow. "What's your name?"

"Kerby Maxwell, ma'am."

"Well, I'm Mrs. Graymalkin, Kerby, and I must say you've been a little gentleman. One doesn't meet many little gentlemen these days. I wish I could do something for you. In fact, you remind me a lot of my Felix when he was your age. Poor little Felix!" she said, and sniffled sadly.

"What's the matter, Mrs. Graymalkin?" asked Kerby. "Did he die?"

"No. He grew up!" she declared, as though this had been quite thoughtless of him.

"Gee, that's too bad," said Kerby.

"I've never forgiven him," she admitted. She laid a bony finger alongside her nose. "In fact, I know what I'll do. I'm going to give you one of his favorite toys, Kerby — one he used to play with by the hour. Do you like magic, Kerby?"

"Sure!"

"And do you like chemistry?"

"Gee, I guess so," said Kerby uncertainly. "I don't know much about it."

"You'll like it," Mrs. Graymalkin assured him. "I'm going to give you Felix's old magic chemistry set. You can do all sorts of flibbertygibbety tricks with it. I'll bring it to the park tomorrow at this same time and give it to you."

"That's very nice of you," said Kerby politely, "but I wonder if you could bring it a little earlier, so I won't be late for supper?"

"Oh? What time do you have supper?"

"The same time as tonight — and I'm already late tonight."

"Oh, my goodness — then I won't keep you. I'll be here tomorrow night at, say, a quarter to six. Now run along!"

"Yes, ma'am!" said Kerby, and sped away with Waldo at his side. "Let's go, boy! We're *really* late now!"

Since they were so late, he decided to take a chance. He would go down Bumps Burton's street and cut through the vacant lot to his yard instead of going over to his own block. With any kind of luck, Bumps would be eating dinner and not bother him.

As he jogged down Bumps's street, he saw Fenton Claypool walking ahead of him. Fenton was new on the block. Only a few weeks ago, his family had moved into the house on the other side of the vacant lot from Bumps.

Fenton was a tall, thin boy who walked very straight, with his shoulders back, and looked at everything in a solemn way without ever changing his expression much. Whenever anybody spoke to him, he replied in a calm, polite way that made him sound smart without seeming prissy. Nothing ever seemed to bother him.

He had a long face, large eyes, and a high forehead. He also had a good-sized nose and big ears that stuck out like cup handles; and yet so far, Bumps Burton had kept his hands off them. For one thing, Fenton had not given him any reason to bother him, since he never made fun of Bumps, not even behind his back, the way the other boys did; and for another thing, Bumps did not know quite what to make of Fenton Claypool. No one did.

When he heard Kerby running up, Fenton Claypool glanced over his shoulder and spoke in his solemn way.

"Hi, Kerby."

"Hi, Fenton."

"What's the hurry?" Fenton fell into step as Kerby reached him, and jogged along at his side. On his long, thin legs, Fenton kept up with Kerby easily.

"Late for supper," panted Kerby.

"Are you going to cut through the vacant lot?"

"Have to."

"But Bumps won't like it —"

"Hope he won't see," said Kerby, turning into the lot. Fenton stopped and watched him.

Over at Bumps's house, the back screen door slammed. Kerby glanced that way again and groaned.

"Hey! Who gave you permission to cut through my lot?"

"I'm late!" cried Kerby, without slowing down any. If anything, he ran a little faster.

"Stop! I wanna talk to you," ordered Bumps. And with Bumps an order was an order. Or at least it was supposed to be.

"Have a heart, Bumps! I can't stop!" Kerby cried over his shoulder.

He didn't know *what* to do, actually.

If Bumps was going to catch him anyway, it would be

better to stop. Maybe then Bumps would let him off with a warning.

But if he stopped, Bumps would make him listen to a lot of talk about staying out of the vacant lot unless he had permission, and then he would be that much later.

On the other hand, in some ways it was not a bad time to stop, because Bumps would not dare get too tough with Waldo around. Waldo was not a large dog, but he was large enough to reach the seat of Bumps's pants if he needed to. Once or twice before, he had growled a low growl at Bumps, just mentioning the fact that he was around, and Bumps had gotten the idea.

Kerby stopped. And as he did, Bumps managed to trip over his own big feet. He went head over heels and skinned his knee.

"I gotta go!" Kerby called, taking advantage of this chance to put distance between Bumps and himself. He ran for the fence, leaving an angry bully sitting on the ground nursing his knee.

"I'll get you, Kerby Maxwell! You got one coming for this!" yelled Bumps. And with these unpleasant words ringing in his ears, Kerby pushed the loose board aside, slipped through the fence, and hurried into his house.

2

KERBY AND WALDO almost did not get to the park at all the next day.

They were in disgrace.

Kerby was in disgrace for being late to supper and for spilling a glass of milk at breakfast and for playing with his food at lunch and for not cleaning up the workbench in the basement as his father had been after him to do for three days now and for standing at the window and sticking out his tongue at Mrs. Pembroke next door when he didn't think she could see him.

As for Waldo, he was in disgrace for chewing one leaf off the avocado plant Kerby's mother was trying to raise (it only had two leaves to begin with) and for wetting on the dining-room carpet and for digging a hole in the flowerbed.

They were not very popular around the Maxwell house just then.

In fact, it had not been a good day at all.

Kerby had to spend all morning making a start at giving the basement a good cleaning. This was a very boring activ-

11

ity on a nice day. To tell the truth, it was a bore on *any* day, but especially on a nice one.

Somehow he didn't get far with it. When his mother came down and saw how much he had accomplished in the way of wasting time, she shook her head severely. She said she didn't know what his father would have to say about it.

This was not true, of course; she *did* know; so did Kerby.

After lunch he still had to stay in, but he sat around where his mother could see him, trying to look pale and unhealthy, so that she would realize how much he needed some fresh air and sunshine.

Finally she took pity on him.

She said well, he could go out and play for a little while, but if he was late for supper again he would not set foot out of the house for a solid week and that was a promise.

"Don't worry, Mom, I won't be late again," he said, shooting out of the door like a rocket. He whistled for Waldo and hurried around the side of the house. He was careful not even to look in the direction of Mrs. Pembroke's house, for fear he might see her and be tempted to stick out his tongue again. He went down his own block to the park, hoping in this way to avoid Bumps.

"Zo-oo-oo-oom! I'm a guided missile!" he declared as he raced along, holding his arms out behind him and leaning

forward. "Come on, Waldo, you be a guided missile, too!" he urged, but Waldo wouldn't try. Waldo was an old-fashioned dog, and he preferred to run in the same old-fashioned way, always.

"The trouble with you, Waldo, is you don't have any imagination," Kerby grumbled, and changed the subject. "Gee, I wonder if Mrs. Graymalkin will really be there?"

Naturally Kerby had said nothing at home about Mrs. Graymalkin and the magic chemistry set she was going to give him. His mother would have said he mustn't take presents from strangers. He could just hear her asking who Mrs. Graymalkin was and where she lived, and wanting to know all about her. He was afraid his mother might not approve of an old lady who acted as strangely as Mrs. Graymalkin did.

Now, however, the closer Kerby got to the park, the more he began to doubt that she would show up at all. In fact, he said as much to Waldo.

"I'll bet she won't come," he said. But even so, he wanted to be there just in case. After all, if she *did* have a magic chemistry set she wanted to give him, he would like to have it.

In the park he met a couple of boys he knew, and Waldo met a couple of dogs he knew, so for a while they simply relaxed and played. Then Kerby remembered about Mrs.

14

Graymalkin and hurried along the path to the drinking fountain.

After a while he began to feel foolish. By then the other boys had gone home. The park was beginning to look deserted. Certainly it looked deserted in the thickly wooded section where he was.

He walked back along the path a little way to look, and he walked ahead along the path a little way to look.

Here came Mrs. Graymalkin, hurrying along with stiff, tottery steps — either she had rheumatism or it was those shoes of hers.

"By golly, Waldo! She really *did* come! But I don't see any chemistry set."

She was wearing the same clothes as yesterday — hat, feather, cape, and all — and when she saw Kerby she smiled. He tried quickly to count how many gaps there were between her teeth. There were at least five or six. There were almost more gaps than there were teeth.

"Well, Kerby dear! I'm glad to see you came."

"Yes, ma'am. Did you —" he began, and then stopped. After all, it wasn't very polite to ask right away if she had brought the chemistry set.

Mrs. Graymalkin cackled. It was her way of laughing, Kerby decided.

"Oh, never fear! I didn't forget it!" she said, patting her

15

cape. Reaching around under it, she produced a long wooden box. "Here's the gift I promised you!"

The outside of the box was plain, but the inside of the lid, when she lifted it, was covered with faded printing in red and black letters:

FEATS O' MAGIC CHEMISTRY SET

Instructive! Entertaining!
Hours of Amusement!
Astonish Your Friends!
Entertain at Parties!
Make Extra Money Giving Demonstrations!

Ranged in a row inside were corked glass tubes full of liquids, each with a faded label on it. One section of the box contained eyedroppers and several glass containers with measurements on their sides — beakers, Mrs. Graymalkin called them — for mixing things in.

There was also a small booklet. The title on its cover was *One Thousand and One Tricks to Do With Your FEATS O' MAGIC Chemistry Set.*

"Gee! That certainly looks interesting," said Kerby, anxious to get his hands on the set.

Mrs. Graymalkin's bony fingers plucked one tube from its place and held it under his nose.

"Here's one of the best ones. My Felix loved to use this one," she said, and Kerby could believe her, because there was not much left in it. "Fill a beaker half full of water. Add two drops of this. The water will start to boil and bubble and steam — but it won't get the least bit hot. You can even drink it down without hurting yourself at all. Everybody will be amazed!"

"They sure will," agreed Kerby, picturing his mother's and father's faces if he pulled a stunt like that. "That sounds like a good trick. I'll try it."

"You do that," said Mrs. Graymalkin, laughing delightedly. "I hope you have fun, Kerby, and I hope we'll meet here in the park again some day, so you can tell me all about it."

"Sure. Gee, Mrs. Graymalkin, thanks!" he said as she returned the tube to its place. She closed the box and handed it to him.

"Carry it carefully!"

"I will. Good-by!" Kerby waved back at her as he hurried away along the walk. "Come on, Waldo!"

Kerby went home, again by way of his own block. As he slipped along the street he watched in all directions. Not only did he want to avoid Bumps, but also he didn't want his parents to see him with the chemistry set under his arm.

They would want to know what it was. Then they would decide it was dangerous and that he couldn't play with it.

It would be better if they didn't know anything about it, he decided; then they wouldn't worry. Maybe later on, after he had gotten the hang of a few tricks, he would give them a show. But for now, the safest thing would be not to let anyone else know about the set.

As he hurried along, Kerby planned his strategy. He had to hide the chemistry set somewhere. The best place for that would be the garage. Somehow he had to smuggle the chemistry set around to the garage without being seen.

He decided he would sneak around the side of his house —the side where the walk did not run. He would crouch low, so that if his parents happened to glance out the windows they would not be able to see him. But then, Mrs. Pembroke might notice him. She seemed to spend most of her time spying out her windows, and she was the kind who would run straight to his mother and tell how she had seen Kerby acting strangely, as though he were up to something She would feel it her duty to tell his mother. She was always feeling her duty.

While Kerby was thinking about this, Waldo suddenly rushed into Mrs. Pembroke's front yard barking wildly and chased her cat up a tree. Mrs. Pembroke had an old cat named Xerxes, and Waldo was constantly chasing Xerxes up trees, and Mrs. Pembroke did not like it. She was always complaining about it.

Kerby could not blame Waldo — that old Xerxes sat around just asking for trouble — but right now was a very bad time to cause a commotion.

"Waldo, cut that out!" he yelled angrily and ran up into his own front yard. As quick as a wink he ditched the chemistry set under the porch, and even then he was not a second too soon. Mrs. Pembroke appeared at her front door and began yelling at him.

"I'm sorry, Mrs. Pembroke," he said, and called Waldo in a stern tone of voice. By that time the fun was over — Xerxes had settled himself in the crotch of a limb well out of reach. Waldo trotted over to Kerby, who gave him a smack on the bottom that didn't hurt any but satisfied Mrs. Pembroke. After she had gone muttering away inside, however, Kerby spoke sharply to Waldo.

"Darn you, Waldo!" he snapped. "Now I'll have to sneak out after dark to get my chemistry set and put it in a safe place!"

They walked on around the side of the house. Through the kitchen windows he could see his mother and father. Kerby glanced at Mrs. Pembroke's windows and saw she was in her kitchen. He decided to take a chance. Quickly he

20

ran back for the chemistry set and sneaked it out to the garage. Once inside, he went to some shelves in one corner. He put the chemistry set on the bottom shelf and covered it with some old rags. There it would be safe until he could find a chance to sneak it into the house and up to his room.

Through the kitchen windows he could see the clock over the stove. Ten minutes till six. He ran into the house. His parents glanced around and were relieved to see that he was not going to get into trouble again tonight.

"Well!" said his mother. "Aren't you the good boy!"

"Sure!" said Kerby, pleased with himself. "What are we having for dinner?"

3

THE NEXT MORNING Kerby waited around the house, watching for a chance to take the chemistry set up to his room. At breakfast his mother had said something about wanting to go shopping that morning. If she did, he would have a chance to play with the set without having to worry.

To stay out of her sight as much as possible, he went into the garage. Waldo came along to keep him company.

As he was walking to the shelves to make sure the set was still there, Kerby accidentally bumped into the lawn mower handle. The lawn mower rolled backwards a few inches, making a noisy grating clatter on the concrete floor as the reel whirled.

"Ssh!" he said fiercely, grabbing it. "Want to get me in trouble?"

If his mother heard the lawn mower, it might remind her to tell him to mow the lawn.

He was crouched down, peeking at the chemistry set and showing it to Waldo, who sniffed it suspiciously, when he heard the screen door slam.

"Kerby!" called his mother.

He covered up the set and came innocently out of the garage as she walked down the back steps. She was all dressed up to go downtown shopping.

"Well, there you are, Kerby. What were you doing?"

"Oh, just looking for something, Mom."

"That garage could use a good cleaning — and when are you going to finish the basement?"

"Aw gee, Mom, do I have to do that today?"

"No, not today," said his mother, pulling on her white gloves.

Kerby felt relieved.

"Today," his mother continued, "I want you to mow the lawn."

"Aw!"

"You heard me. It's been needing it for days. If you finish before I get back, you may go play in the park — but only after you've finished. And you're not to go anywhere but to the park. Either go to the park to play or stay here and play in the back yard. I won't be gone very long. Now get started on the lawn. I want to see you start before I leave."

Grumbling about his lot, Kerby rolled the lawn mower outside and began pushing it up and down the yard while his mother was backing the car out. She waved and told him to do a good job and drove off.

As soon as she was gone, Kerby gave the lawn mower a good kick.

"*That's* for reminding her," he told it, and sat down in the grass to think. Before he cut any more grass, he decided, he would take the chemistry set to his room.

Once there, he put it on his desk and examined everything in the box. He tried to read the labels on all the tubes and uncorked each one for a sniff. All the chemicals smelled either funny or awful, and two or three made his eyes water. Waldo sneezed and left the room, looking disgusted. Furthermore, he refused to come back. Kerby went after him, and even dragged him part way along the hall by his tail, but Waldo struggled and escaped from him.

"Oh, all right, *don't* come back," said Kerby, and returned to his room alone.

After he had examined the beakers, he sat down on his bed and read about some of the thousand and one tricks in the booklet. They sounded so exciting it was hard to believe they would really work. After a while he decided that before he went back to his lawn-mowing he would try just one trick.

He remembered what Mrs. Graymalkin had told him about how to make water bubble and boil without its becoming hot. That sounded like a good trick.

He could not even read the name of the chemical she had

said to use for that trick. The label was too old and faded. But at least he was able to pick it out again because the tube was the one that had only a small amount left in it.

He uncorked the tube again for another sniff. It had an odd smell. Mostly it reminded him of wet sneakers left overnight in a small closet.

Kerby took a beaker to the bathroom and filled it half full of water. Returning to his room, he placed it in a wire stand that came with the set. Next he opened the same tube again and thrust an eyedropper into it. Holding the eyedropper and tube high where he could watch closely, he carefully pulled a tiny amount of the liquid into the eyedropper.

Kerby felt very scientific.

"That ought to be about two drops," he said to Waldo, forgetting that Waldo had left.

He turned to the beaker half full of water. Carefully, holding his breath, he squeezed the chemical into the water.

Nothing happened.

No bubbling.

No boiling.

No steaming.

The water just sat there doing nothing. It was very disappointing. Kerby flopped down on his bed with an angry bounce.

"Aw heck! Might know her old chemistry set would be a

26

fake!" he muttered, thinking hard thoughts about Mrs. Graymalkin.

After brooding for a moment, he sighed and decided to empty the beaker in the bathroom. After that he would try a couple of the other tricks, just to see if any of them would work. Probably the chemicals were old and had lost all their fizz, but maybe some of them were still good. He might as well try. While he was experimenting with the chemistry stuff, he could think of some excuse for not mowing the lawn.

As he walked down the hall he held the water up to the strong light pouring through the window at the end of the hall. The water was clear and not smoking or bubbling or boiling or steaming even a little bit. He sniffed it to see if the chemical gave it any smell.

Kerby stopped. The water had a strangely delightful, irresistibly tempting scent. Before he knew what he was doing, he obeyed a powerful urge.

He lifted the beaker to his lips and drank its contents. The instant he did this, Kerby was scared.

He remembered all about *Dr. Jekyll and Mr. Hyde,* and what had happened to Dr. Jekyll when he got to messing around with *his* chemistry set. Dr. Jekyll had drunk some stuff he mixed up, and the next thing he knew he had changed into a horrible, hairy man who went out and did all sorts of terrible things. It made him bad, very bad.

With a scared cry, Kerby rushed into the bathroom and looked at himself in the mirror. Would he change into a monster before his very own eyes? Would his face get all hairy and his teeth turn into great fangs?

All he saw in the mirror, however, was his own pale face. It was about six shades whiter than he had ever seen it before, but nothing else was different about it.

He stuck out his tongue, half expecting to see little toadstools growing all over it, but it looked all right too.

Then all at once his eyes rolled in circles, twice, and a strange feeling overcame him.

He felt good.

That was the only way to describe it. Good. Very good.

When Waldo had heard Kerby's scared cry, he must have thought his master was really in trouble, because he came running loyally to see what was the matter.

By the time he arrived that good feeling had come over Kerby. He was rinsing out the beaker and drying it on a paper towel. Waldo stared up at him inquiringly. Kerby gave him a kind and affectionate smile. He stooped and patted his best friend gently on the head.

"Waldo, I want to apologize for dragging you down the hall by the tail," he said. "That is a mean thing to do, and I won't do it again. Besides, your nails scratch Mom's floors. In fact, they may already have done so from time to time.

Later on I must remember to polish the floors for her."

Waldo reared back and gave his master a worried look. Kerby threw the paper towel in the wastebasket, being careful to see that it dropped in and did not litter up the bathroom floor. Then he returned to his room, with Waldo padding after him.

"I must put away my chemistry set now and not try any more experiments with it up here in my room," he told Waldo as he put away the beaker and closed the box. "After all, this is no place to play with chemicals — I might spill some and mark my furniture. Why, I didn't even spread any newspapers on my desk before I started! Besides, this is no time to be fooling around playing. I have work to do."

So saying, Kerby went outside and finished mowing the lawn. After he had finished mowing, he trimmed the grass around the trees and along the back fence. Then he raked up all the grass and put it on the compost heap.

When his mother came home, she found him down in the cellar finishing up his cleaning job there.

"What a wonderful job you did on the lawn!" she said, coming downstairs to stare at him in amazement. "I never saw such a job!"

"I was glad to do it, Mom," said Kerby.

"And now, to find you working down here — Kerby, do you feel all right?"

"I feel good, Mom," he said. "Very good."

"Well . . ." His mother still looked doubtful, but she rose and started upstairs. "I'll fix some lunch, and —"

"It's already fixed, Mom," said Kerby, causing his mother to stumble on a step and nearly fall on her face, she was so surprised. "I thought I'd have it all ready for you when you came home."

After lunch he worked in the basement again all afternoon. Every once in a while his mother called down in an anxious tone to make sure he was all right. Around three o'clock she even telephoned his father and had a long conversation in a low voice with him.

When Kerby finally came upstairs, his father had just come home from work. Mr. Maxwell looked at him in a nervous way and laughed a hollow laugh.

"Well, son! Well . . . What have you been doing today?" he asked in what was probably supposed to be a jolly tone of voice.

Kerby told him.

His parents glanced at each other.

"Kerby, I want to take your temperature," said his mother, heading for the downstairs medicine chest with a determined step.

Now, ordinarily Kerby would have bucked like a steer at the idea of having his temperature taken, or swallowing a pill, or anything like that. But this time he simply smiled in a perfectly agreeable way.

"If you want to, Mom, please do, but I really do feel good. Very good."

His mother took his temperature. It was normal. She and his father stood around handing the thermometer back and forth and staring at it as if they didn't believe it.

"Maybe we should call the doctor anyway," said Mrs. Maxwell.

"Well . . . let's wait and see what develops," said Mr. Maxwell. "I'd feel like a fool, talking to a doctor about . . . about . . . I don't even know what about!"

"I'm perfectly all right," Kerby assured them. "Want me to set the table, Mom?"

"Why . . . yes, I guess so," gasped his mother, hardly able to believe her ears. Kerby was already busy washing his hands so that he could take out silverware for the table.

After dinner, at which he was very careful about his manners and did not spill any milk or play with his food one little bit, Kerby offered to dry the dishes.

"No, thanks! No!" said his mother, almost crying. "Go out and play. You've done enough work for one day. I want you to go out and play."

"May I go to the park?"

"Yes!"

"Thanks, Mom. I'll be home before dark."

Kerby ran over to the park, where he was very nice to all the other children and even called hello to Bumps Burton in such a friendly fashion that Bumps was completely confused and astonished. He watched with his heavy lower jaw flapped open while Kerby went past. Bumps was busy playing ball at the time, so he didn't bother to chase after him.

Before dark, Kerby was home again.

"Do you want to watch television awhile?" his mother asked.

"No, I think I'll go up and start reading a book for my summer book report," he told her and ran upstairs. The clatter behind him in the living room was the sound of his father's pipe falling out of his mouth.

That night, when it was his bedtime, Kerby did not go to bed and read comic books with a flashlight under the covers as usual. This time his light went out promptly, and Kerby settled down immediately.

"After all," he murmured to Waldo, who was keeping a worried vigil on the rag rug nearby, "a boy my age needs his sleep."

4

"KERBY! TIME FOR BREAKFAST!"

Kerby opened one eye, and sunlight streamed into it, making him squint and close it again. He rolled over and cautiously opened the other eye, remembering immediately everything that had happened yesterday. All the work he had done and everything.

"Kerby?"

"Yes, Mom."

It was his mother calling from downstairs. The way her voice sounded, you could tell she was wondering what to expect from him this morning.

Kerby wondered himself.

He sat up carefully in bed, terrified for fear he might feel the urge to start doing more chores. As he sat checking himself, he heard the rattle of Waldo's toenails on the stairs.

"Come here, boy!"

Waldo came into the room, but not with his customary rush, and he didn't jump up on the bed for a roughhouse the way he usually did. Instead, he sidled into the room with a worried expression on his muzzle and cocked his head at Kerby, looking him over.

Kerby climbed out of bed and walked over to him. All at once he reached down, grabbed Waldo by the tail, and spun him around.

Waldo yelped joyously, and for a moment they battled wildly. Waldo was so pleased he raced up and down the hall and in and out of every room, skidding on every turn and scattering small rugs all over the place.

Kerby was pleased, too.

"Well, I guess I'm all right," he decided, and quickly dressed in his tee shirt and shorts and sneakers.

When he came down for breakfast he walked into an uneasy atmosphere. Both his parents looked at him in a funny way. His father cleared his throat and put down the morning paper.

"Well, good morning, son," he said. "By the way, while I think of it — I understand your mother mentioned to you yesterday that the garage could stand a good cleaning —"

"Aw gee, Pop, do I have to do it today?" asked Kerby.

His father sat back and glanced at his mother. They both looked relieved.

"No, no, not today, son," Mr. Maxwell assured him. "Just some day. You did quite a job around here yesterday."

Kerby's mother put her hand on his forehead.

"He's perfectly normal," she announced happily.

"Good!"

"I guess it was just another phase," she said. Whatever Kerby did, they always seemed to say he was "going through a phase." It was one of those things parents say about children.

"I'm okay, Mom," he assured her.

After his father had left for his office, Kerby's mother went over to a neighbor's house for coffee. That gave Kerby a chance to go back up to his room and look at his chemistry set again.

Naturally, he had realized the terrible truth about that stuff he had mixed up and drunk.

It had made him *good*.

It had made him be good and do good deeds all day. But at least its effects seemed to last only one day. A good night's sleep cured the condition. Kerby shuddered to think what it would have been like if the condition had been permanent, if it had made him be good forever!

Now that he knew, though, he was extremely curious. He was curious to know if the stuff would really work the same way twice — only on somebody else!

"Who can I try it on?" he wondered.

At that moment Waldo came trotting into the room. Kerby looked at him and smiled.

"Waldo!" he said, jumping up and taking out a beaker and an eyedropper. "Stick around, boy — I've got something for you!"

He filled the beaker half full of water and returned to his room, shutting the door so that Waldo could not leave. A couple of minutes later he had everything ready. In the meantime, Waldo had become uneasy and was scratching at the door to get out. Kerby walked slowly across the room toward him, holding out the beaker.

"Nice Waldo! Come on, boy, have a nice drink!"

Waldo backed into a corner. Whenever Kerby called him "Nice Waldo" in that gooey tone of voice it was time to be on guard.

"Here, boy! It won't hurt you. Look, it's nice," said Kerby, and sniffed at the beaker to show Waldo it was all right and smelled good . . .

Too late, he knew he had made a mistake. The aroma had an unearthly fascination. Unable to resist, Kerby raised the beaker to his lips . . .

When his mother came home an hour later, she was startled to see a cloud of dust coming out of the garage. She peeped in to find Kerby slaving away with a broom.

"Kerby!" she squeaked. "What are you doing?"

"Cleaning the garage, like Pop said to," replied Kerby.

"But he didn't say you *had* to!"

38

"I'm glad to do it, Mom. It really needs it. By the way, have you got any floor wax?"

"Floor wax? Now listen, Kerby, there's no need to wax the garage floor —"

"I wasn't going to. I was thinking of the hall floor upstairs. Waldo's scratched it up pretty badly, running back and forth, so I want to polish it for you."

Mrs. Maxwell tottered inside and went straight to the telephone to call her husband. He agreed that this thing had gone far enough and that they had better have Dr. Murad come over for a look.

So Dr. Murad came over, and Kerby had to interrupt his work to stick out his tongue and say ah-h, and have his chest thumped and his heart listened to, but Dr. Murad couldn't find a thing wrong.

"I tell you, Mom, I feel good," Kerby insisted. "Very good."

"He keeps telling me so," his mother remarked to Dr. Murad, "but it's hard to believe."

The two of them went into another room and muttered together the way doctors and mothers do.

"Keep him under observation, and let me know if there's any change," the doctor told her and went away.

Kerby cleaned the garage and polished the floor in the upstairs hall and set the table for dinner, and that evening he finished the rest of the book for his book report before it was time to go to bed.

He was perfectly happy, but his parents and Waldo all went tiptoeing around looking as gloomy as if he were dying of some strange disease.

The next morning, instead of just calling him, his mother came all the way upstairs to wake him up.

"Well!" she said, when he had opened his eyes. She laid a cool hand on his forehead. "How's our little man this morning?"

Kerby wondered about that himself. It was too soon to say. He sat up slowly in bed.

"Well, I'm okay, I guess," he said finally, "but I've sure had enough work for a while!"

"Would you like to stay in bed and just rest this morning?"

"No, I'm okay. I feel like going over and playing in the park," said Kerby — and he was delighted to discover that was the way he really did feel!

5

THE MAIN REASON he wanted to go to the park, of course, was to look for Mrs. Graymalkin.

He wanted to see her again. He was very anxious to ask her some questions. How come the trick didn't work the way she said it would? Why didn't the water bubble and boil? Why was it the chemical smelled bad in the tube but good when you put only two drops of it in some water? Had it ever made her son Felix be good and do a lot of chores, the way it had him? There were lots of things he wanted to ask her.

He stayed in the park all morning, walking around and looking everywhere, but Mrs. Graymalkin never appeared.

When he went home for lunch, he even looked in the telephone book to see if he could find out where she lived, but she was not listed.

Not since yesterday had he touched the chemistry set. Actually, he was afraid of it. Anything that could make him do chores all day long for two days in a row was powerful stuff indeed, and something to be extremely careful with.

42

After lunch he returned to the park and played there most of the afternoon, until he saw Bumps. He was ready to go home anyway, so he whistled for Waldo and drifted away from the gang he was playing with before Bumps could see him.

He was ready to go home because his curiosity about the chemistry set was beginning to overcome his fear, and he wanted to experiment with it some more.

His mother was gardening in the back yard. She looked concerned when she saw him returning home so early.

"What's the matter, Kerby? Don't you feel well?"

"Sure, Mom. I just have some things I want to do."

"You mean some — er — work?" his mother asked anxiously.

"No, I just want to fool around."

"Oh. Well, all right."

He went on inside, realizing he would have to be extremely careful this time. It would scare his poor mother to death if he started working away at chores a third day in a row. She would have Dr. Murad come back and would make all kinds of fuss about it.

Up in his room he took out the chemistry set and filled a beaker half full of water. Then he tied a large bandanna handkerchief over his face, Western bandit style. What he really needed was one of those masks doctors use when they

43

operate on people, but since he didn't have one, he had to make the bandanna do.

Next he went to work with the eyedropper and extracted a couple of drops of chemical from the glass tube. Carefully he dropped them into the water. And even though he had the handkerchief on, he still held his breath.

Waldo had been racing up and down the newly polished hall floor, enjoying skidding on the turns. He had come in now to sit down and rest a minute, and was watching his young master curiously.

When Kerby glanced at him, Waldo stood up and began to leave in a hurry. Kerby grabbed him by the collar and shut the door. He dragged Waldo over to the table and seized the beaker, still holding his breath. He was about to burst from holding his breath, and Waldo was twisting and straining, trying to get loose. Desperately Kerby stuck the beaker under his nose.

Waldo stopped struggling. He sniffed the water twice, and then began lapping it out of the beaker with his pink tongue. Slurp! Slurp! Slurp! — and it was all gone.

"Pah-h-h-h!" said Kerby, letting out his breath in one big burst. He yanked the bandanna off his face and sat down on his bed and gasped for a while.

At the same time he watched Waldo carefully to see what would happen.

The first thing that happened was that Waldo's soft brown eyes rolled around in circles, twice. Then he stood up with his paws on Kerby's knees and licked his hand adoringly.

Next he trotted out into the hall. Kerby put away the chemistry set and followed him.

At the end of the hall a small rug had been knocked into a heap by one of Waldo's wild dashes. When Kerby came out, Waldo had one end of it in his mouth and was pulling it back where it belonged.

"My gosh!" gasped Kerby. "The stuff works!"

When he had finished straightening the rug, Waldo trotted downstairs. Kerby followed eagerly.

Waldo trotted out onto the front porch just in time to see Xerxes prowling around over in the yard next door. Automatically, without thinking, Kerby said the same thing he always said when they saw Xerxes.

"Sic 'em!" he muttered in a low voice Mrs. Pembroke could not have heard even if she had been listening.

Waldo looked up reproachfully at his young master and sat down.

Xerxes saw him and his back went up.

"Yeow!" sneered the cat, daring Waldo to give him a chase.

Waldo's pink tongue lollygagged out of the side of his mouth, and he gazed at Xerxes in a friendly fashion.

The cat sat down and stared at him in amazement.

"I can't believe it!" said Kerby, echoing what must have been Xerxes' own thoughts on the matter. Kerby sat down beside Waldo to feel *his* head. "Are you all right, boy?"

Waldo licked his hand reassuringly.

After Xerxes had puzzled over Waldo's odd behavior for a moment, and had tried to figure out what his next-door enemy might be up to this time, the big cat rose and strolled with a great show of indiffcrence to the very edge of the boundary between the two yards. He stood for a moment, his tail twitching back and forth, watching Waldo narrowly out of the corners of his green eyes.

Waldo returned his gaze with gentle good humor.

Xerxes became desperate. He liked a little action when Waldo was around. Xerxes was very good at climbing trees and it gave him a chance to show off. So now he did a very daring thing. He walked *onto Waldo's property,* strolled straight to *Waldo's favorite tree,* stood up lazily, and *sharpened his claws on it!*

Kerby was scandalized.

"Waldo!" he cried. "Are you going to let that cat sharpen his claws on *your tree?*"

Waldo gave his master a look that as much as said, "Why not?"

"Well, for Pete's sake!" snorted Kerby, and stamped inside the house and up to his room. He was disgusted. This was going *too* far! For two cents he would have kicked that old chemistry set out the window. The only thing that stopped him was the knowledge that Waldo would be all right tomorrow, after a good night's sleep.

At least, he *hoped* he would!

Wouldn't it be awful if it didn't work that way on dogs? If it was permanent?

"Oh gosh, why did I try it on Waldo?" groaned Kerby in an agony of remorse. "Why didn't I try it on someone that doesn't matter, like Mrs. Pembroke?"

After a while his father came home from work. Kerby ran downstairs in time to hear him talking to his mother in an astonished tone of voice.

"What's got into that crazy dog?" he was asking. "If it isn't one thing around here, it's another!"

"What do you mean? What's the matter with Waldo?" said Kerby's mother.

"Don't ask me — but do you know what he was doing just now when I turned into the drive? He was out there in front pushing dirt back into that hole he dug in the flower-bed!"

"What?"

"Not only that, he was patting it down with his paw!"

Mrs. Maxwell stared at her husband for a moment and then turned toward the telephone.

"We'd better call the veterinary."

Kerby thought fast.

"Maybe he'll be all right tomorrow, Mom. Maybe he's going through a phase."

His mother stopped and blinked at him.

"Don't be silly, Kerby. Dogs don't have phases. Or do they?" she added in a less certain tone of voice.

The Maxwells exchanged a helpless glance.

"Kerby's right. Let's wait and see," said Mr. Maxwell finally, and Kerby breathed easier.

6

IT WAS A HOT SUMMER'S MORNING. Kerby stood out on his back porch, thinking.

Two days had passed since Waldo had spent the day being a good dog, and in all that time Kerby had not even touched the chemistry set again.

Every minute he could he had spent in the park. Both afternoons he hung around the drinking fountain, hoping to see Mrs. Graymalkin again, but she never appeared.

In the meantime, he had let the tubes and beakers alone for a while.

He had been very relieved, yesterday, when morning came and Waldo was back to normal again. He had chased Xerxes up a tree and chewed the other leaf off the poor avocado plant and wet on the living-room rug and dug a new hole in the flowerbed.

So for a couple of days now, Waldo had been acting normal, and Kerby had been acting normal, and Mr. and Mrs. Maxwell had stopped worrying. Maybe dogs *did* go through phases, they decided; at least they stopped worrying about it.

Now, however, as he stood out on the back porch, Kerby began to feel a return of scientific interest in his chemistry set.

What caused this was the sight of Bumps Burton, over in his back yard.

Bumps was beating a rug for his mother. He had it hung across a clothesline, and he was whacking it now and then with one of those wire rug beaters.

Bumps was stripped to the waist, and the perspiration was running down his back like a river. After about every three whacks he stopped and mopped at his face with a rag.

His mother stuck her head out the window and scolded him.

"Bumps Burton, you get to work on that rug! I want it really beaten!"

"Okay, okay, I'm working, ain't I?" Bumps replied in a sulky tone.

Still thinking about one thing and another, Kerby watched him for a while. Ever since Bumps had fallen over his own feet and skinned his knee, Kerby had managed to avoid him. But he would not be able to do so much longer.

Tomorrow was pageant practice for the boys' choir at church.

Just about every boy in the whole neighborhood was in

the boys' choir — including Bumps. In fact, Bumps had a big part in the pageant. He was Pugnius the Roman Centurion. He was the head of the Roman soldiers, and he was to come in pulling along Humilius the Christian Martyr.

Tomorrow they were going to rehearse at the church. Miss Pease, the church organist and choir director, was going to direct them as usual, and Kerby knew he would have to be there.

If he had only been First Roman Citizen, Second Roman Citizen, or Third Roman Citizen — all small parts, or better yet, merely one of the Roman Mob like all the rest of the boys, then maybe Kerby could have gotten away with not going. But the trouble was, he had a big part, so he knew his mother would insist on his going to rehearsal.

Kerby was to be Saint Securius the Rescuing Angel. All the boys had drawn lots to see who would play Saint Securius — and Kerby had lost. He was stuck with the part, fair and square.

This meant he would have to show up the next afternoon for sure. Yet if he did, one thing was certain: sometime during that long afternoon Pugnius the Roman Centurion would find a chance to twist the nose of Saint Securius the Rescuing Angel.

"If only I could do something about Bumps *before* then," he muttered to himself.

And he began to get ideas.

Presently he turned and went into the kitchen.

"Mom, can I have some lemonade?"

"Mom, *may* I have some lemonade," Mrs. Maxwell retorted.

"Okay, Mom, may I?"

"Yes, you may. There's some already mixed in a bottle in the refrigerator."

Kerby poured himself a glass and took it upstairs. He brought out the chemistry set and put on the bandanna. After he had added two drops to the lemonade, he took off the bandanna and, carrying the lemonade at arm's length, returned downstairs.

He was crossing the kitchen on his way out when his mother, who was peeling potatoes at the sink, glanced around at him.

"Whew!" she said, wiping her forehead with the back of her knife hand. "How about giving me a sip of that?"

Kerby's heart skipped a beat.

"Gee! I — can't!" he said desperately.

"Why, what a little pig!" said Mrs. Maxwell. "Do you mean to say you won't give your poor old mother one dinky sip of your lemonade?"

He had to think of something, and he did.

"A fly got in it!"

"Oh. Well, why didn't you say so? Pour it out."

Kerby poured the lemonade down the drain in the sink. He hated to do it, but there was no other way out.

Mrs. Maxwell drew in her breath deeply as the lemonade went down the drain.

"My goodness, that smells heavenly! Pour me another glass, please, will you?"

"Sure, Mom," said Kerby, and poured two fresh glasses.

He drifted away upstairs with his, and when he came down this time he went out by the front door, taking no chances.

Once outside, he walked around to the back yard and over across the vacant lot toward Bumps Burton's house. He was nervous, but at the same time he felt so confident he didn't even whistle for Waldo to come along.

Between the listless whacks he was giving the carpet, Bumps glanced around and saw him.

"Hey!" he said, throwing down the carpet beater and looking glad to see Kerby — glad in a mean way, that is. "What are you doing in my vacant lot?"

It wasn't his vacant lot at all, but he always talked as though it were.

"Hi, Bumps," said Kerby. "I just wanted to watch you work."

"Yeah? Maybe I don't want any little squirt watching me.

Anyway, you've got something coming for being a wise guy," he declared, advancing on Kerby in a threatening manner.

In spite of himself, Kerby's knees were shaking. He managed to smile.

"Aw, take it easy, Bumps. Here, you can have my lemonade," he said, holding out the glass.

Bumps stopped and looked at it thirstily. As hot as he was, the frosty glass must have looked very desirable. With an ill-tempered grunt, he took it from Kerby.

"You're darned right I can have your lemonade," he sneered.

Lifting the cool glass, Bumps drank greedily. He drank every bit of it. Every drop of it.

He lowered the glass and licked his lips.

"Boy! That was good. But don't think you can get off the hook that easy. You've *still* got one coming," said Bumps, turning nasty again.

As merciless as a steel clamp, Bumps's fingers went for Kerby's nose.

"Aw, cut it out, Bumps!" quavered Kerby, backing away. Too late it occurred to him — maybe the stuff didn't work in lemonade!

"Come here, you!" snarled Bumps, grabbing him by the neck. "I'll teach you not to —"

Suddenly Bumps's mean eyes rolled around in a circle, twice.

He blinked.

Then he began to smile pleasantly. The unfriendly hand around Kerby's neck relaxed its grip and became a friendly hand on his shoulder.

"Gee, Kerby, that lemonade was swell. Here!" Bumps fished around in the pocket of his shorts and brought out a dime. "Here, take this. I want you to have it. There's no reason you should give me your lemonade for nothing."

"G-goshalmighty!" gasped Kerby, accepting the dime and the empty glass.

Waldo had suddenly appeared, as though he had sensed his master might be in danger. He looked up at Bumps with surprise.

"Well, thanks, Bumps," added Kerby.

"Thank *you*, Kerby," said Bumps. He glanced around with a noble look on his face. "Well, I've got to get back to work. We've got a lot more rugs that ought to be beaten after I finish that one, and besides that, I haven't straightened up my room. See you later, Kerby. So long, Waldo!" he said, stooping to stroke Waldo's head and give him a friendly pat on the back.

Waldo was so astounded he didn't even growl. Bumps turned and trotted back to his own yard, where he picked up the rug beater and began whaling away at the rug as though there were nothing he liked to do better.

For a moment they simply stood and stared at Bumps.

"I'm as surprised as you are, Waldo," Kerby whispered. Then he called, "You don't mind if we watch you work, do you, Bumps?"

Bumps waved cheerily.

"Certainly not, Kerby!"

After a while he finished beating the rug. Taking it off the line and rolling it up neatly, he carried it into the house.

A couple of minutes later he came staggering out under a huge load. He must have been carrying at least six rugs.

Behind him came his mother. She looked like somebody walking in her sleep. Kerby distinctly saw her give herself a good pinch.

"Sure, Mom, I'm fine. I feel good. Very good," Bumps was telling her over his shoulder.

"Waldo! Did you hear that?" whispered Kerby. "That's exactly what I said to *my* mother. I said, 'I feel good. Very good.'"

"I'll get started on these rugs, but when you're ready to go to the store, Mom, let me know, and I'll go with you. I don't want you to have to carry any heavy bundles," said Bumps.

Mrs. Burton stood on the back porch goggling after him, with her mouth opening and closing like a goldfish's. She

58

was speechless. Finally she turned and went inside without a word.

At first Kerby simply stood there and enjoyed himself, watching Bumps Burton work. After a while, however, Kerby's happy smile began to fade. He returned thoughtfully to his own yard and sat around, worrying.

First he sat on the back steps and worried. Then he moved around to the front steps and worried.

Waldo went with him both places, but he merely lay in the grass and snoozed. One thing Waldo never bothered to do was worry.

While Kerby was worrying, he happened to glance up the street and see Bumps Burton again. Bumps, who was carrying a heavy sack of groceries for his mother, had stopped to help an old lady across the street — and he wasn't even a Boy Scout!

Kerby watched him and groaned.

As he remarked to Waldo, "Well, it's all right for now — but what'll happen tomorrow when he wakes up mean again?"

7

THE NEXT MORNING when Kerby opened his eyes, this is how he felt about waking up: he hoped he hadn't.

"I hope I'm just dreaming I'm awake," he muttered. "I hope I'm still asleep and it's not tomorrow yet."

But then Waldo came scrambling into the room and jumped up on the bed and licked his nose, and Kerby knew the sad truth. It was morning.

A few hours from now he would be wearing that ridiculous long white robe and those pasteboard wings and that silly pasteboard halo taped onto a stick. The boy who was Humilius the Christian Martyr would be wearing another long robe and a sorrowful expression and would have a rope around his neck. Bumps Burton would be wearing pasteboard armor and shin guards and a helmet covered with gold paper, and he would be carrying a wooden sword painted with aluminum paint to look almost exactly like steel if you didn't look too closely, and he would have Humilius' rope over his shoulder and be pulling Humilius along by it.

He would also be biding his time. Watching for his chance. Keeping his fingers ready for nose-twisting.

Thinking about this, Kerby wrinkled his nose in a sniffle. He sniffled in hopes of discovering that he had a bad cold, a terrible cold, and would have to stay in bed all day.

Unfortunately, however, his head seemed to be perfectly clear.

He thought a little bit about trying to twist his ankle, but decided that might be too hard to do on purpose.

He listened to see if he could hear his mother's footsteps downstairs. He wondered what time it was and knew it must be late. Last night she had said she thought he looked a trifle pale and tired, and that she wanted him to sleep later than usual in the morning.

He slipped out of bed, went to the window, and looked out. Sure enough, his mother was outside, working in the flowerbed, getting ready to fix up the place where Waldo had dug a hole.

Kerby sat down in a chair and turned his problem over in his mind for a few minutes. Then he went to his closet. There he burrowed around in a corner and brought the magic chemistry set out of its hiding place.

He carried it to his desk, opened the box, and took out the special tube. Kerby held it up and looked at it, and after a

61

while he began to look less worried. He glanced around at Waldo.

"Waldo, I've got an idea. But I'll need your help," he said. "The point is this: if two drops of this stuff makes anybody be good until he gets up the next morning, would just a tiny bit make him be good for a couple of hours? I want to find out."

Kerby sneaked downstairs to the kitchen. He picked up Waldo's water dish and carried it carefully upstairs. Waldo, who had accompanied him, trailed along watching curiously.

Setting the dish down on his desk, Kerby took out the special tube and an eyedropper, put on his bandanna, and dropped a single tiny drop of the chemical into Waldo's water. Just the tiniest bit.

After stirring the water with a pencil that happened to be handy, Kerby set the dish on the floor.

"Here, boy. Have a drink," he urged.

Since Kerby had not grabbed him by the collar or anything, Waldo had not become too suspicious concerning what was going on. Besides, dogs have short memories, and he had probably forgotten all about the other time. Be that as it may, however, he did not seem to be thirsty at the moment, and probably had no intention of drinking any of the water — but what he did do was to sniff it curiously, as any dog would have done; and that was what Kerby had been counting on.

Waldo took one sniff, and that was that. He began to drink the water with noisy slurps, and he didn't stop until it was all gone.

His eyes rolled in circles, twice. He leaped up to lick Kerby's hand adoringly. Then he turned and trotted out of the room and downstairs.

Just then the telephone rang. Kerby rushed to the window and saw his mother get up off her knees, out alongside the flowerbed, and come inside to answer it.

"Want to come out? All right, come on," Kerby heard her say to Waldo on her way in, and knew she was holding the door for him.

Waldo trotted down the back porch steps and straight to the flowerbed, where he began pushing dirt back into the hole he had made and patting it down with his paw.

"I'm glad somebody called Mom to the telephone!" muttered Kerby. He pushed his head against the screen. "Waldo! Come back here!" he cried, and hurried downstairs to let him in.

Waldo came obediently, like a *good* dog, a *very good* dog, the instant Kerby opened the door.

"Come upstairs!" ordered Kerby, and hurried him upstairs

in front of him. He took Waldo into his room and shut the door.

"Now! I want you to stay right here until this stuff wears off!" he declared. "Sit!"

Waldo sat.

"At least it makes you do what you're told," observed Kerby.

He climbed back into bed and watched Waldo closely.

"Come here, boy," he said. "Jump up here."

Waldo gave his master a reproachful glance. He was not supposed to jump on the beds, not even Kerby's — even though he always did — and he knew it. Being a good dog for the moment, he was horrified by the suggestion.

Downstairs, Kerby's mother finished her telephone call and came to the foot of the stairs.

"Kerby!"

"Yes, Mom?"

"How do you feel this morning?"

"All right, I guess."

"Good. I wouldn't want you to miss your pageant rehearsal."

"I know, Mom."

"Get dressed and come downstairs and have your breakfast."

"Yes, Mom. I'll be right down."

Slowly, Kerby dressed. As he did, he kept watching Waldo.

For a long time, Waldo continued to sit in his corner being a good dog. Finally, however, he gave his head a shake and looked around him with a confused expression.

Kerby sat down on the bed.

"Come on, boy! Let's wrestle!"

With a bound, Waldo leaped up on the bed, and they wrestled. Waldo was a normal dog again.

"Gee, that's swell, Waldo!" declared Kerby. "It lasted for a little while, but not too long. Now maybe I can work things out all right this afternoon!"

8

AFTER HE HAD EATEN HIS BREAKFAST, Kerby went out into the back yard to fool around and to think some more about what he would do that afternoon. By then his mother had stopped gardening and gone inside, so that he and Waldo were alone in the yard.

They had not been there long before Fenton Claypool came out of his house. Being careful to walk around the edge of the vacant lot, he cut across the back yard next door and came over.

"Hi, Fenton."

"Hi, Kerby. Hello, Waldo," said Fenton, patting Waldo on the head. "Kerby, I want to ask you about something."

"What?"

"Well, yesterday I was looking out of my window and I saw you come out of your house and walk over toward Bumps. He was beating a rug. I thought you must be crazy, letting yourself in for trouble that way. But then you gave him a glass of something, and he drank it, and a minute later he started acting funny. Very funny," said Fenton, giving

Kerby a deep, solemn glance that was full of meaning. "Kerby, what made him act that way? What was in that glass?"

Kerby's eyes grew round. He stared at Fenton Claypool with something like awe.

"How did you know it had anything to do with my — my lemonade?"

"What else could it be?" replied Fenton. "Why, I could see his eyes sort of roll around, and — Lemonade, you say?"

"Yes."

"But not ordinary lemonade, that's for sure!"

Kerby stared at Fenton Claypool and came to a swift decision. Fenton seemed like a good guy, and one he could trust. And with all his brains, maybe Fenton could clear up something that had been bothering him — What made the magic chemical work the way it did? Was it really magic, and was Mrs. Graymalkin a — a —

"Listen, Fenton," said Kerby.

"Well?"

"Listen, Fenton. You want to hear something? Something crazy? Something you won't be able to believe?"

"Yes!" Fenton nodded eagerly. "That's why I came over."

Without ever taking their eyes off one another, they sat down in the grass.

"Okay, I'll tell you exactly what happened," declared Kerby, and began at the beginning. He told Fenton all about meeting Mrs. Graymalkin in the park, and about the magic chemistry set she gave him, and about what had happened to him and to Waldo when they had drunk water with the magic chemical in it.

Fenton ate up every word. In fact, he almost smiled as he listened. His eyes sparkled joyfully. He was excited and delighted. Quite plainly, nothing could have pleased him more than to be in on something as unusual as this was. And Kerby was glad to have someone to tell his story to. He was tired of having such a big secret penned up inside him, with nobody to share it.

When he had finished, Kerby asked the question that had been burning in his mind ever since he had first discovered the strange effect of the magic chemical.

"Fenton, do you think it's really magic?" he asked. "And do you think — er — well, what do you think Mrs. Graymalkin is?"

He hesitated as their eyes met intently, and then he came out with it.

"I mean, do you think she's a *witch?*"

Fenton Claypool's head went back in amazement. Then he actually did smile. In fact, it would not be going too far to say that he chuckled.

"A *witch*? I should say not, Kerby! I certainly don't believe there actually are such things as witches."

"Well, neither did I — until I met Mrs. Graymalkin,' Kerby pointed out.

"Just the same, I'll bet she's nothing but an eccentric."

"A what?"

"An eccentric."

"What's that?"

"That's somebody who acts sort of nutty, but isn't really crazy but only odd. I think she's just odd. And I don't think your magic chemical is really magic, either. Listen, Kerby, would you let me see your chemistry set? I've had several of them myself, and maybe I can —"

"Sure! Come on! Only don't say anything about the set to my mother. My parents don't know I have it."

"That's best," declared Fenton. "If they knew you had it, they'd be sure you'd blow yourself up with it or something, and they'd take it away from you."

"That's exactly what I figured," agreed Kerby, liking Fenton more every minute. "Come on up to my room!"

It was a good thing Kerby had warned Fenton not to say anything about the set, because his mother was in the kitchen when they came inside.

"Well! Hello, Fenton. I'm glad to see you boys getting together," she said.

70

"Good morning, Mrs. Maxwell. It's nice of Kerby to ask me in," replied Fenton politely, bowing a little to hide the twinkle in his eye. Fenton was the sort of boy mothers were all too likely to call "a perfect little gentleman," but Kerby decided not to hold it against him. After all, Mrs. Graymalkin had called *him* a "little gentleman," he recalled with a squirm.

"I want to show him some of my things, Mom," said Kerby.

"That's fine. Run along upstairs."

Twenty seconds later Kerby had the chemistry set out on his desk and his visitor was carefully inspecting the special tube.

Fenton Claypool squinted narrowly at the liquid in the tube and pressed his lips together thoughtfully.

"H'm. Very interesting, Kerby. Too bad we can't read the label. All right if I smell the stuff?"

"Sure. In the tube it's all right — but two drops in a beaker of water or a glass of lemonade — oh, boy! It's funny, too, because in the tube it just smells like wet sneakers."

"Or old goldfish-bowl water," suggested Fenton, sniffing the contents of the tube. "H'm. Interesting."

"Well, what do you think?"

"Well, in the first place, this set looks very old."

"Yes, I guess it is. It belonged to Mrs. Graymalkin's little

boy, and any little boy *she* ever had must be pretty old by now. Besides, she *said* he's grown up."

"All right. Then it's very old. So old we can't even read the label any more. Now, do you know what happens to chemicals sometimes when they become very, very old?"

"No, what?"

"Some of their properties change."

Kerby had been expecting some exciting announcement. He stared at Fenton, puzzled.

"So?"

"Well, think of it!"

"I *am* thinking of it. But what does it mean?"

"Oh. Well, it means that some of the things that make up the chemical change, so that *it* changes into something different. It isn't exactly the same as it used to be, and it doesn't work the same way any more."

"Oh! I see what you mean!" Now Kerby was excited. "Gosh, Fenton! You think that could be it?"

"I'm sure it could. So what we've got to do is take this to a chemist and have it analyzed, so we can find out exactly what it *is*. Gee, Kerby, I think we ought to go right away! Come on, let's look in the telephone book —"

"No, wait, Fenton! We can't take it anywhere now — we've got to go to pageant rehearsal right after lunch. And anyway, I want to use it today."

"What?" Fenton came close to looking surprised. "Use it? Today?"

"Yes. Because of Bumps, mostly," replied Kerby, and explained his idea. "You know how Miss Pease's refreshments committee always brings a pitcher of lemonade for us to have after we've finished rehearsing. And you know how a few of the kids — especially Bumps — always sneak out into the kitchen when she's not looking and snitch a glass of lemonade *before* we start. Well . . ."

"Yes, I know — but if you put some in the whole pitcher, then when we're finished they'll *all* have some, and —"

Fenton paused to stare at Kerby in a questioning way. A guilty grin burst on Kerby's face like a Fourth of July rocket in the sky.

"Well, I thought it'd be fun to see what they'd all do!"

Fenton Claypool thought this over thoroughly. Then he sat down on the bed and proved that for all his brains he was completely human. He slapped his bony knee and nearly laughed his head off.

"Gee whillikers! That ought to be worth seeing! Wowee!" he cried, and fell back on the bed holding his stomach and kicking his long, thin legs in the air. "Oh golly, Kerby! I sure want to see that!"

9

THE REHEARSAL was to take place in the parish house at the church. Kerby and Fenton showed up early. For one thing, Kerby knew that if he waited until later Bumps might get there first and be laying for him outside. For another thing, they wanted to watch for a chance to do the lemonade trick. Whenever they had a chance, they would slip the drops into the lemonade.

Since he had only a small part — he was Third Roman Citizen — Fenton persuaded Kerby to let him carry the special tube.

"You're Saint Securius, and you have to jump around some," Fenton pointed out. "Something might happen to the tube if you kept it in your pocket."

When they arrived, one of the refreshments committee mothers was carrying in a big pitcher of lemonade and a covered tray of cookies. They held the door open for her, and exchanged a glance as they watched her walk into the kitchen.

"Later," muttered Fenton.

In the main room, a costumes committee mother was hanging the costumes up on a coat rack. Miss Pease's pageants were always organized that way, down to the last detail.

Miss Pease herself was already there, of course, and buzzing around the room like a June bug. She had a narrow face, no chin to speak of, and protruding eyes that gave her a startled expression. In fact, other people's surprised looks were Miss Pease's regular looks.

When she directed the annual pageant she was always terribly earnest about it. She got pink in the face and had a straggle of hair that kept falling down on her forehead. Every so often she would push it back up with her long, thin hand, but it soon fell down again.

As soon as she saw them come in, she began waving her hands and giving orders.

"All right, Third Roman Citizen, get into your costume! Saint Securius, put on your robe. The sooner we get started with Costume Check, the better."

Once parts had been assigned and rehearsals began, she never called anybody by his own name but always by his name in the pageant. And she always had special names for everything they did. Trying on costumes to see if they fitted was Costume Check; moving through the action of the pageant the first time was Action Blockout; having cookies and lemonade when they were finished was Refreshments Break, and so on. They were expected to know all of Miss Pease's special terms and jump when they heard them like soldiers jumping for bugle calls. In fact, the way Miss Pease sang them out, they *sounded* like bugle calls.

Helped by the costumes committee mother, Kerby and Fenton Claypool tried on their costumes and found they fitted pretty well. Even Miss Pease, who buzzed in their direction to give them an inspection, was satisfied. Of course, Kerby felt extremely foolish in his costume, with his pasteboard wings and with his head encircled by a gold band, from the back of which sprouted his halo on a stick. But that could not be helped.

Fenton Claypool's costume was a Roman toga, the same as most of the other boys'. The toga looked like a white sheet, which was not surprising, since it was made out of half of an old one. The toga was worn over one shoulder and under the other arm. For good measure, the Roman citizens had each been given wreaths to wear around their heads. Miss Pease said this was very much the style with Old Romans. Kerby looked enviously at Fenton's toga and wished he were wearing one too.

While they were trying on their costumes, other boys began to arrive. One of them was Bumps Burton. When he

saw Kerby, he gave him a mean look. Mean and somewhat puzzled. He grabbed Kerby by the arm and pulled him away from the crowd trying on costumes.

"Hey, cut it out, you're bending my wings!" protested Kerby.

"Shut up. I wanta talk to you, see?" growled Bumps under his breath. "Come out in the kitchen."

"Nothing doing!"

"I ain't gonna touch you — yet. I just wanta ask you a couple of questions about something that happened that's mighty, mighty funny. Something that happened to me," he added, glaring suspiciously.

"Why — er — what — uh —"

"*You* know what I mean! Yesterday —"

"Pugnius! Don your armor!" cried Miss Pease, with her own special brand of fierce gaiety, as she swooped down on Bumps. "Come, come, Roman Centurion, you have more costume to put on than anybody!"

"Okay, okay," said Bumps, but before he left he grabbed Kerby, pulled his ear so close to his mouth that Kerby thought he was going to bite it off, and hissed, "If you don't want your nose twisted like a doorknob, you meet me in the kitchen right after Costume Check!"

He gave Kerby a quick, sharp shake that made his halo

tremble, and then shoved him aside and stalked away to put on his costume.

Kerby smoothed down the front of his white angel robe and went looking for Third Roman Citizen. He looked everywhere without success, until finally he thought to look in the kitchen.

Fenton Claypool was there, fidgeting impatiently.

"I thought you'd never come, Kerby! Now's our chance!" Reaching under his Roman toga, he pulled the tube out of his pocket and handed it to Kerby. "Put the drops in the lemonade while I keep watch at the door."

"Okay! Now, I'm just going to put in two drops for the whole pitcher."

As quickly as his shaking hand would permit, Kerby uncorked the tube, held his breath, and shook two drops into the lemonade.

"There!"

"Done?"

"Yep!"

"Give me the tube!"

Fenton sprang away from the door, took the tube, and returned it to his pocket. Kerby looked around for something to stir the lemonade with, saw nothing, and stirred it with his finger.

"Hey, guess what?" he said as he stirred. "Bumps grabbed

me and wants to talk to me. He knows there was something funny about the lemonade I gave him. Gee, I hoped he was too dumb to figure that out!"

Fenton Claypool shook his head.

"I don't believe he's as dumb as you kids all think. He's big and awkward and talks funny, but —"

"Well, anyway, he told me to meet him out here in the kitchen after Costume Check or he'd twist my nose like a doorknob."

"Like a doorknob?" Fenton chuckled appreciatively. "Not bad. Imaginative. Really, I think Bumps might surprise you if you ever gave him a chance."

"Huh! It's all right for you to stand around and laugh — you're not the one that's going to have your nose twisted," said Kerby. He stopped stirring the lemonade and licked his wet finger. "But he's liable to come in here any minute, and I don't know what to say when he does."

"Let him come," said Fenton confidently. "He'll be sure to snitch a glass of lemonade the very first thing, and — Hey! What's the matter?"

Kerby's eyes were rolling. When they stopped, his face assumed an angelic expression that went well with his costume.

"Fenton, I'm surprised at us, trying to pull a silly trick on the boys at a time when poor Miss Pease is working so hard to put on a nice pageant," he declared. "I'm going straight to her and tell her what we've done and apologize for —

"Come back here!" cried Fenton, seizing him by the robe and yanking him back into the kitchen.

"Please, Fenton. It's the right thing to do."

"Kerby! Snap out of it, Kerby!" cried Fenton, holding onto him tightly and giving his cheek several small slaps. Kerby blinked and shook his head. His expression changed to one of puzzlement.

"Hey, stop smacking me! What — Oh, my gosh! Did I —"

"Yes. You shouldn't have licked your finger!"

They both gazed at the lemonade pitcher with awesome respect.

"Gee, that's really powerful stuff," remarked Kerby. "Still, a lick only lasted a few seconds, so a glass should last a few minutes. And before it wears off, we'd better disappear."

"We will. We'll — Oh, hello, Bumps!"

A grunt from the doorway announced that Bumps had arrived. His helmet and his armor glittered and his steel-like sword was in his hand.

"Huh! It's lucky for you you're here, Kerby Maxwell!" he declared. He shook a warning finger at Kerby as he stepped into the kitchen. "Now, I wanna know —"

"First Run-through!" The bugle call rang out sweet and clear. "Places, everybody, for First Run-through!"

82

"Aw nuts!" Bumps hesitated. "Well, we gotta get out there for First Run-through or she'll come looking for us. But as soon as we've finished First Run-through I wanna see you right back out here again, you hear me?"

"Okay, okay, Bumps," said Kerby, exchanging a glance with Fenton. "Come on, let's go before old Pease-and-Carrots catches us out here."

They hurried into the main room and took their places for First Run-through. Over at Costume Check, the costumes committee mother was struggling with the large gray robe of an unhappy-looking small boy named Jimmy Pratt, whose expression was exactly right for his part.

"Hurry up, Christian Martyr!" cried Miss Pease, slinging an impatient glance in the direction of Costume Check. "What's keeping our Humilius? Humilius, I do hope this is the *last* time you'll be late for rehearsal!"

"Yes, ma'am," said Humilius, with proper Christian meekness.

"*Please* hurry up!" insisted Miss Pease.

At this, the costumes committee mother threw up her hands and whirled around angrily.

"We *can't* hurry up! There's something wrong with this costume — it's miles too big! I don't know *what* Agnes Millikan was thinking of when she made it, but she certainly wasn't thinking of Jimmy Pratt!"

Miss Pease darted over like an aroused dragonfly.

"What? Too big . . . ?" She dragged the folds of the robes this way and that, making sure how much was empty robe and how much was Jimmy Pratt. No doubt about it, there was a lot of empty robe around. Standing with the robe sagging all about him on the floor, he looked like a half-melted candle.

Miss Pease rolled up her eyes in anguish, pushed the straggle of hair off her damp forehead, and groaned.

"Really, this is the *last* year I'm going to do a pageant, the very *last* year!" she declared. "The lack of co-operation I get is — is — Well, we've no time to cry over spilt milk. We'll have to have a new Christian Martyr, that's all. A tall one," she decided, casting her eye about the group. It fell upon the tall, straight figure of Fenton Claypool.

"Third Roman Citizen! Change costumes with Humilius — at once! His robe will fit you, and we can make your toga work for him!"

10

THERE WAS NO ARGUING with Miss Pease — but then, Fenton Claypool was not the kind of boy who argued, anyway. Nothing ever seemed to bother him, no matter how unexpected it was. Here was one of the biggest parts in the pageant being handed to him, with lots of lines to learn and with Bumps Burton on the other end of a rope around his neck, and yet he never turned a hair.

"Yes, Miss Pease," he said, and began taking off his toga. He was one cool cucumber, Kerby thought admiringly. As for Jimmy Pratt, he looked relieved at the idea of not having to be dragged around by the neck by Bumps Burton. He had been living in terror for days, wondering how hard Bumps would yank.

When the boys had exchanged their costumes, First Run-through began. The main idea of the pageant was simple. Pugnius the Roman Centurion appeared dragging along Humilius the Christian Martyr. He was leading Humilius to the arena to be thrown to the lions. (Two of the boys were Lion Roars off stage.)

As Pugnius and Humilius appeared, the Romans lined the way to jeer at the Christian Martyr. Suddenly, on a platform behind them, Saint Securius the Rescuing Angel appeared. Parting the crowd with his wand as he came down through it, Saint Securius stood in front of Pugnius and made a short speech, during which he not only saved Humilius but converted Pugnius to Christianity. Pugnius fell on his knees before Saint Securius and asked for his blessing. Then he rose, removed the rope from Humilius' neck, and the three of them marched out together singing "Onward, Christian Soldiers" while the Romans fell on their knees in amazement.

Every year Miss Pease thought up something like that for the annual pageant. She had been doing it for twenty-six years.

First Run-through did not go too well. The new Humilius knew most of his lines already, just from listening at rehearsals, but Saint Securius and Pugnius each forgot about half of theirs.

"Dreadful! *Simp*-ly dreadful!" declared Miss Pease, buzzing around in a fury. "We'll rest for exactly three minutes — Don't leave the room! — and then try it again! Some of you Romans looked like absolute ragbags! You don't know the first thing about how to wear a toga! I want all Romans to assemble here in front of me for Toga Practice!"

This gave Kerby and Fenton a chance to slip out to the kitchen again. And a moment later, Bumps came sneaking in.

He glowered at Fenton Claypool.

"Who asked *you* to be here?"

"I wanted some lemonade."

Bumps stalked over to the lemonade with a forbidding frown on his large, heavy face.

"Nobody's having any lemonade around here but *me,*" he declared, pouring himself a glass. "And then I want to ask you a couple of questions, Kerby Maxwell!"

Fenton Claypool inspected the menacing bully with genial admiration.

"I'll say one thing, you look every inch the Roman Centurion, Bumps," he declared.

"Huh!" said Bumps. He couldn't help sounding the tiniest bit pleased at this compliment. "Who asked you?"

He raised his glass. Then his eyes narrowed, and he stopped.

"Hey! That was lemonade you gave me before, Kerby! You done anything to *this* lemonade?" he asked, sniffing it suspiciously.

Of course, once he sniffed it, he was lost. It was too late to stop. He put the glass to his lips and drank.

"Ah-h! Boy, was I thirsty!"

He set the glass down. Then, once more, he remembered about the other lemonade.

"Why, you little rat!" he snarled and stepped toward Kerby.

Too late.

His eyes rolled. A friendly smile spread across his face. He glanced around at the lemonade and looked ashamed of himself.

"Gee, fellows, I shouldn't have snitched that lemonade. That was an unfair thing to do. *One* of us shouldn't have any until *all* can have some," he declared. "I'm going right out and tell Miss Pease and ask her to forgive me."

After politely asking them to excuse him, Bumps marched out of the kitchen to tell Miss Pease he had been a bad boy. Kerby watched him go, and giggled as he turned back to Fenton.

His giggling stopped abruptly when he saw what Fenton was doing.

"Hey!" he cried, alarmed.

Fenton Claypool was pouring out a glass of lemonade.

He glanced at Kerby with a smile.

"I want to try this myself."

"Fenton! Are you nuts?"

"No. I just want to find out for myself what its effects are really like."

"Don't be crazy!"

"A dedicated scientist never hesitates to experiment on himself," declared Fenton, "and I'm a dedicated scientist. Or anyway, I'm going to be one when I grow up."

A new thought comforted Kerby.

"Oh well, go ahead," he said. "It probably won't have any effect on *you,* anyway — you're already good. How can you get any better? Why, if you drink that, nobody will even notice the difference. So go ahead."

"All right, I will," said Fenton, and drank the glass of lemonade in one long, continuous swallow.

He put down the glass and waited.

"Are my eyes rolling?"

"No . . . Yes! There they go!"

"Second Run-through!" The shrill notes rang from the walls. "Places, everybody, for Second Run-through!"

"Fenton! Are you all right?"

Fenton Claypool smiled strangely.

"Sure."

"Then come on! There's old Pease-and-Carrots calling!"

"Nuts to her," muttered Fenton with another strange smile, but allowed Kerby to pull him along by the hand. He also allowed the rope to be put back around his neck as he took his place for Second Run-through, but Kerby noticed uneasily that he was still smiling in that peculiar way. Sort of sinister, it was.

"All right, now, let's go!" cried Miss Pease, clapping her hands sharply. "Pugnius!"

"Yes, Miss Pease?" said Bumps sweetly.

"Lead on Humilius!"

"Yes, Miss Pease. Ready, Humilius?" he asked, glancing back with a friendly smile as he put the rope over his shoulder.

"Shut up and get going," replied Fenton.

Bumps looked hurt by this rude response, but he turned and gently led Fenton forward.

"I hope I'm not hurting you?" he called anxiously over his shoulder.

"No, and you'd better not," snapped Fenton.

"Pull harder, Pugnius! It has to look rougher than that," Miss Pease pointed out. "And Humilius, try to look a little meeker and more long-suffering!"

"Ha!" jeered Fenton.

Hiding behind the platform on which he would soon appear, Kerby peeked around the side of it in amazement. What on earth was wrong with Fenton Claypool?

Suddenly it dawned on him.

There was only one answer to the way Fenton was acting.

He was already good, and now he had drunk some stuff that made people good. Obviously, it was too much for him.

"Gosh! This is going to be *terrible!*" muttered Kerby. He was almost afraid to watch.

Dutifully, in obedience to Miss Pease's order, Pugnius yanked harder on the rope, causing Humilius to stumble.

"That's better!" applauded Miss Pease. "That looked real!"

"That *was* real!" snarled Humilius, on his hands and knees. "Cut that out, you big bum!"

"Oh, I'm sorry!" declared Pugnius, rushing back to help the Christian Martyr to his feet. Several of the Romans snickered uncertainly.

"Ha!" With a savage jerk, Humilius yanked the rope loose from around his neck. "You'll be sorrier than *that* when I get through with you!"

And so saying, the Christian Martyr grabbed the Roman Centurion's sword out of his hand and gave him two tremendous whacks on the helmet!

All the Romans cheered wildly. They thought this was a great improvement on the pageant story. But Saint Securius thought enough was enough.

"Hey, stop it, Fenton!" he cried, rushing forward.

Humilius turned on him with a most unmartyrlike air.

"Oh, you want some too, huh? Take that!" he cried, and lopped off a wing with his sword.

"Stop it, I say!" yelled Saint Securius, trying his best to duel him with his wand, but Humilius broke it in two with a single stroke, and then the other angel wing went flying. Kerby ducked just in time, or Fenton's third swing would have sliced off his halo.

Next Fenton started chasing Bumps Burton all around the hall while the other boys cheered and Miss Pease let out a wail and collapsed into a chair.

Out the door went Pugnius, with Humilius close behind him, and all the Romans behind *him*. Hoisting up his long angel robes, Saint Securius finally took out after *them*.

"Hit him again! Hit him again!" cried the Romans, anxious to see Bumps Burton get it good for once.

But then Fenton Claypool's Christian Martyr robe tripped him up and he went sprawling. Bumps kept on running, however, and the other boys ran after him. Kerby stopped to help Fenton.

Fenton sat up, shook his head, and looked confused.

"What happened? . . . Oh! Oh!" he groaned, as he remembered.

"Fenton! Are you all right?"

"Yes. I'm myself again, if that's what you mean," he said. "Say, I was pretty bad, wasn't I?"

"You sure were! Gee, I had no idea —"

"Hey! What are they doing?"

As usual, Bumps had finally fallen over his own feet, and the other boys had caught up with him. They had all piled on him, and their fists were flying.

Fenton sprang to his feet.

"Here now, that's not fair!" he protested. "Bumps won't fight back, so they'll beat the stuffing out of him!"

"You're right! Come on, we've got to help him!" cried Kerby.

They rushed to the rescue.

"Cut it out, guys! Leave him alone!" yelled Kerby, pulling one boy off the pile.

"Stop it!" ordered Fenton, pulling off another. The boys were so surprised that by the time they got over their surprise, Kerby and Fenton had pushed them all away and were standing between them and Bumps, who was holding his head and looking dazed.

"Hey, what do you think you're doing?" shouted one boy angrily. "He's got it coming!"

"But it's not fair, all of you piling on him! Especially not when he's — when he's — er —"

How could you explain?

"Get out of the way!" yelled someone.

"No!"

"Then we'll *knock* you out of the way!" yelled a second boy, and the whole gang rushed them.

11

KERBY AND FENTON did the best they could, but they were rapidly getting the worst of it when all at once the enemy started tumbling in all directions.

Bumps was on his feet again, and he was making short work of the other Romans. As they scrambled up after a push in the face from Bumps, all the Romans started running back to the parish house as fast as they could run. Soon Bumps and Fenton and Kerby were standing alone.

Bumps stared at them in a wondering way.

"How come you guys were fighting those guys?"

"Because they were beating you up," said Kerby.

Bumps gave him a scornful look.

"You're kidding! Why would you stop them from beating *me* up?"

"Because it wasn't fair. There was stuff in that lemonade that made you be good. You wouldn't fight back, so you didn't have a chance."

"When we put the stuff in the lemonade, we certainly didn't mean for you to get beat up," said Fenton. "I drank some, too, but it had a different effect on me. It made me mean. So I started the trouble. But then I fell down and got over feeling mean, and by then the other kids were beating up on you."

Bumps scratched his head.

"I don't understand," he muttered.

"I don't blame you. It's kind of crazy, but —"

"You put some dope in the lemonade, huh?"

"That's right, Bumps. And it made you act good. So when the other kids started beating up on you, it wasn't fair, and we tried to stop them."

Bumps stared at them in amazement.

"You mean you were on *my* side?"

"Yes."

"Huh!" Bumps leaned down, picked up his dented helmet, and put it on while he thought this over. "Nobody's ever been on *my* side before," he remarked.

"Well, *we* were."

"Huh!" said Bumps thoughtfully. Then he wrinkled up his nose and sniffed. "Hey, what's that funny smell?"

Both Kerby and Fenton became aware of an odor that smelled like wet sneakers. Or old goldfish-bowl water.

"Oh, golly!" Fenton felt the side of his robe. It was wet. Hiking it up out of the way, he gingerly turned his pants pocket inside out. Flakes of glass fell out of it. "The tube!"

98

"My magic stuff!" wailed Kerby.

They stared at each other in dismay. Even Fenton Claypool was so upset it took him a moment to gather his wits together. But then he snapped his fingers.

"The lemonade!" he cried. "We've got to get the lemonade! It's our last chance to find out what the chemical is! Come on!" he urged, and raced back toward the parish house. Kerby raced after him, and Bumps followed.

"What's the matter? Whatcha want the lemonade for?" Bumps asked as they caught up with Fenton alongside the parish house. Fenton had crouched down below window level. He motioned for them to crouch down, too.

"Tell you later!" he whispered. "Right now we've got to peek in the kitchen window and see if we can sneak in and grab the lemonade!"

They crept to the kitchen window and peeked in. The lemonade pitcher was sitting on a table.

Empty.

Kerby and Fenton Claypool exchanged a silent glance and then moved without a word to the next window.

The sight that met their eyes would have made a wooden Indian gasp.

"Criminee!" whispered Bumps. "What's going on in there?"

Miss Pease looked dazed. Pinky Marshall was politely

holding a chair for her. Eddie Mumford and Bruce Carmichael were politely helping her into it. All the other boys were brushing each other off and straightening each other's togas.

"Don't worry, Miss Pease, we'll do anything you want us to do to make the pageant a success, won't we, fellows?" Buzzy Dugan was saying — Buzzy, who never did anything but gripe!

"Sure we will!"

"I'll be glad to play Saint Securius if you want me to, Miss Pease!"

"So will I, Miss Pease! We'll make this the best pageant ever, just you wait and see!"

Bumps was dumfounded.

"What the heck is the matter with those guys?"

"It's the lemonade trick," sighed Kerby.

"You mean the lemonade made 'em act that way?"

"Sure. They came back thirsty from running and fighting, and they all gulped down a glass of lemonade, and — Well, we might as well get out of here. They sure won't need us for any more rehearsal *today!*"

Quietly they stole away.

"Gee!" marveled Bumps as they walked down the street. "You honestly mean that stuff made 'em act that way? And you ain't got any more of it?"

"No," said Kerby, and sighed again.

"Too bad!"

Bumps glanced from one to the other of them then with a funny, pleased expression on his bruised face. He looked almost shy.

"You guys really *were* fighting on my side, huh?" he remarked.

"Sure!"

"Huh!" Bumps sounded as though he just couldn't get used to the idea — and all at once Kerby realized something:

This guy had never had anybody on his side before! That was what was wrong with him!

"Hey, I got an idea," said Bumps. "You know that vacant lot in between our houses? What say we build ourselves a clubhouse there?"

Kerby and Fenton's eyes met in astonishment.

"You mean it?"

"Sure! I always wanted to," Bumps admitted, "but heck, it's no fun having a club with nobody else in it."

"Swell! Let's have a club!" cried Kerby.

"Count on me!" said Fenton.

"And we won't let those other punks in," growled Bumps.

"Not right away, anyway," said Fenton. "Not until they want to be friends."

Bumps frowned over this idea for a minute.

"Well, maybe," he said finally. "We might let in a few later on, if they act right."

Planning their clubhouse, they hurried on toward home, and after a while they felt so good they wanted to sing. Arm in arm, the Christian Martyr with the ripped robe, the battered Roman Centurion with the dented helmet, and the black-eyed Rescuing Angel with the clipped wings and the cockeyed halo rehearsed their big number:

Onward, Christian soldiers,
Marching as to war-r-r! . . .

The magic chemical was gone, the lemonade trick was lost forever. But still — Kerby couldn't help thinking — it had worked out better than most tricks did, at that!

About the Author

SCOTT CORBETT is the author of many other Trick books about Kerby and Fenton, including *The Disappearing Dog Trick*, *The Hairy Horror Trick*, *The Hangman's Ghost Trick*, and *The Mailbox Trick*, all available as Apple Paperbacks. Mr. Corbett lives in Providence, Rhode Island.

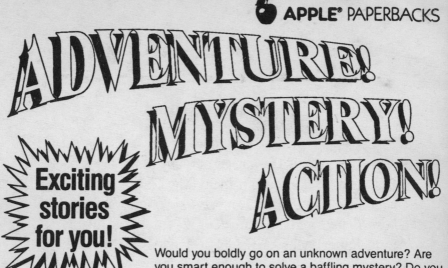

🍎 APPLE® PAPERBACKS

ADVENTURE!
MYSTERY!
ACTION!

Exciting stories for you!

Would you boldly go on an unknown adventure? Are you smart enough to solve a baffling mystery? Do you love nonstop action? Then these Apple books are for you! They're packed with all of the things you love and more. Best of all, they're *fun*! So go ahead, pick an Apple and polish off some great reading.

Apple titles:

☐ MN40691-4	**Computer That Said Steal Me, The**	Elizabeth Levy	$2.50
☐ MN41836-X	**Custer and Crazy Horse: A Story of Two Warriors**	Jim Razzi	$2.75
☐ MN42513-7	**Fast-Talking Dolphin**	Carson Davidson	$2.75
☐ MN42463-7	**Follow My Leader**	James B. Garfield	$2.75
☐ MN40937-9	**Kavik, the Wolf Dog**	Walt Morey	$2.75
☐ MN32197-8	**Lemonade Trick, The**	Scott Corbett	$2.50
☐ MN40565-9	**Secret Agents Four**	Donald J. Sobol	$2.50
☐ MN42414-9	**My Secret Identity**	Jovial Bob Stine	$2.75
☐ MN41830-0	**Mystery of the Haunted Trail, The**	Janet Lorimer	$2.50
☐ MN41001-6	**Oh, Brother**	Johnniece Marshall Wilson	$2.50

Available wherever you buy books...or use the coupon below.

Scholastic Inc. P.O. Box 7502, 2932 E. McCarty Street, Jefferson City, MO 65102

Please send me the books I have checked above. I am enclosing $_____
(please add $1.00 to cover shipping and handling). Send check or money order—no cash or C.O.D.'s please.

Name_____

Address_____

City_____ State/Zip_____
Please allow four to six weeks for delivery. Offer good in U.S.A. only. Sorry, mail order not available to residents of Canada. Prices subject to change.

AB 389